George Henry Calvert, Jared Sparks

Arnold and Andre

An Historical Drama

George Henry Calvert, Jared Sparks

Arnold and Andre
An Historical Drama

ISBN/EAN: 9783337335144

Printed in Europe, USA, Canada, Australia, Japan

Cover: Foto ©Andreas Hilbeck / pixelio.de

More available books at **www.hansebooks.com**

ARNOLD AND ANDRÉ.

AN

HISTORICAL DRAMA.

BY

GEORGE H. CALVERT,

AUTHOR OF "SCENES AND THOUGHTS IN EUROPE" AND "THE GENTLEMAN."

BOSTON:
LITTLE, BROWN AND COMPANY.
1864.

RIVERSIDE, CAMBRIDGE:
STEREOTYPED AND PRINTED BY H. O. HOUGHTON.

PERSONS REPRESENTED.

AMERICAN.

GEORGE WASHINGTON, *Commander-in-Chief.*
Major-General ARNOLD.
Mrs. ARNOLD, *his Wife.*
Colonel HAMILTON, *Aide-de-Camp to General* WASHINGTON.
Major McHENRY, *Aide-de-Camp to* LAFAYETTE.
Major VARICK, *Aide-de-Camp to* ARNOLD.
JOSHUA SMITH, *friend of* ARNOLD.
PAULDING, ⎞
WILLIAMS, ⎬ *Captors of* ANDRÉ.
VAN WART, ⎠
Sergeant BRIGGS.
FLEMING.
VANBERG.
Old Man.
His Grandson.
Farmers, Citizens, Attendants.
Major-General GREENE, *President,* ⎞
Major-General, MARQUIS LAFAYETTE, ⎬ *Members of the Court of*
Major-General, BARON STEUBEN, ⎪ *Inquiry.*
General KNOX, *and ten others,* ⎠

BRITISH.

Sir HENRY CLINTON, *Commander-in-Chief.*
Colonel BEVERLY ROBINSON, *an American Tory.*
Major ANDRÉ.
Captain SUTHERLAND, *Captain of the sloop-of-war "Vulture."*
Old British Officer.

SCENE: *Up the Hudson River, except the 2d Scene of Act* I., *which is in New York.*
TIME: *From September* 18th *to* 30th, 1780.

PREFACE.

An historical drama being the incarnation —
through the most compact and brilliant literary
form — of the spirit of a national epoch, the
dramatic author, in adopting historic personages
and events, is bound to subordinate himself with
conscientious faithfulness to the actuality he at-
tempts to reproduce. His task is, by help of
imaginative power, to give to important conjunc-
tures, and to the individuals that rule them, a
more vivid embodiment than can be given on
the literal page of history, — not to transform,
but to elevate and animate an enacted reality,
and, by injecting it with poetic rays, to make it
throw out from itself a light whereby its features
shall be more clearly visible.

Historic subjects have necessarily an epic bias,

events sweeping men along in their current, instead of the current being much determined by the personalities of men. Hence Shakspeare's most dramatic tragedies, *Macbeth* and *Lear* and *Hamlet*, are drawn from the prehistoric period, where the poetic as well as the dramatic genius has freer scope; while those from English and Ancient history are enjoyed for their clean characterization and luminous historic picture-painting, and for — what is common to all his work — great thoughts buoyed on a sea of beauty, more than for the prolific interplay of feelings and the deep entanglements of passion — inextricable but by death — and the breadth of seemingly free movement, which make the tragedies wrought by Shakspeare out of legend a glowing epitome of the fallible and pathetic in human nature, a poetic abstract of the tragic liabilities of man. The Epic may be likened to a broad, swollen, majestic, irresistible river : the Dramatic to the pent-up waters of a rock-bound lake lashed by a tempest.

But the Dramatic, gathering up the varied and separate impulses of humanity into condensed organic wholes, combines into itself both the other classes of poetic utterance, perfusing its tissue with lyric as well as with epic juice. As Shakspeare's historic plays are largely tinted with epic color, others so sparkle with fantastic wilfulness that they may almost be styled lyrical dramas ; foremost among which are *Midsummer Night's Dream* and the *Tempest*, wherein, through scenes and dialogue still thoroughly dramatic, Shakspeare has more completely than elsewhere given vent to his poetic and, I may venture to say, his personal individuality, saturating them with the inmost fragrance of his beautiful nature, and making them buoyant with the fullest play of a divine cheerfulness.

To get a view of the level little enclosure of the three acts that are to follow, it is not at all necessary to ascend to these Shakspearian heights, up to which one is ever tempted by the fruit that grows on them, — a golden crop, inex-

haustible in its beauty and healthful succulence. We come down from them to say, that the momentous consequences involved in success or failure, the exciting and special nature of the incidents and accompaniments, the individualities of the two chief agents, with the figure and character of Washington looming in the background almost like a controlling destiny, give to the treason of Arnold rare capabilities as an æsthetic subject; and if the necessary locking of the plot within a few breasts, and the separation of the principal agents except for one interview, prevent there being much of that action and reaction between the personages which is needed for the deepest dramatic involution, this is largely compensated for by the contrast between the natures of Arnold and André, and by the direct effect which their personal qualities and temperaments had on the original conception of the treason and on its issue.

Although, from the confined circle in which such a treason necessarily moved, it be not as a subject for dramatic treatment the richest and broadest, it is nevertheless well fitted for such treatment, inasmuch as not only its inception and progress, but also its defeat, were so directly the result of the especial character of the several persons engaged. The epic flow pauses for a moment while human passions enact this episode. In the rising stream of our history an eddy was made to which a high military trust enabled a Major-General to give so wide a sweep that the success of his plot would have caused the current disastrously to overflow, if not to change entirely its channel.

The aim of the dramatist being to reproduce in poetic form a chapter or section of National Annals, and fidelity therefor to the spirit of the period selected being a primary condition to the attainment of his aim, it follows that truth of characterization becomes a demand which he must satisfy, or fail in his undertaking; for the events, owing their import, and it may be their very existence, to the individualities of the chief historic agents, the more faithfully these are re-produced the more truly will the historic spirit be preserved, it being the peculiar quality of epochs fitted for dramatic treatment, that their spirit is a distillation, so to speak, out of that of the influential agents, in a measure the creators, of the epoch. By truth of characterization is meant historic truth, which is not only no bar to poetic truth, but makes for it a solid elastic basis, history and poetry enlivening and elevating one the other. Poetry being the finest truth, the essence indeed of truth, nourishes itself ro-bustly and palatably on the true, pines if fed on the false, and has within itself such all-sufficient resources, that whatever is required for its own corporeal manifestation it can freshly generate, if need be, by imaginative energy. Wherefore, to falsify history in order to compass dramatic ends, were in the author self-conviction of incompe-tency; and whenever such falsification has been resorted to, it will be found that there is weak-ness in the spirit, as well as in the body, of the product.

But to compass his ends, the dramatist may "feign according to nature," not only in the dialogue and monologue of the historic figures, but also by intermingling with them others, the breath of whose life is the concentrated spirit of the epoch represented. Such inventions are not justifiable merely, as being in keeping with the historic picture: they are demanded for the very purpose of giving to historic fact more palpable actuality. They are not mere ornaments, — for as such they would be vicious weaknesses, — but are serviceable adjuncts, which, by not only harmonizing with the known personages, but by giving higher relief to them and their deeds, heighten and enlarge the dramatic effect. Being secondary, they are like the flying buttresses of a cathedral, which, although subordinate, give to the edifice strength, as well as grace and expansion. This dramatic privilege I have used, especially in the first and second Scenes, seeking by means of it to bring more clearly to view the public and military opinion and feeling of the

time, and by thus exhibiting the medium in
which the transactions occur, and by which they
are subtly influenced, to impart to the dramatic
picture more fulness and vivacity.

Whether or not Mrs. Arnold knew of her husband's design was for some time uncertain. I
believe that the final judgment upon all the evidence accessible is, that she did not. I should
in every case have eagerly seized upon and given
her the benefit of any doubt, as to suppose her
ignorant is grateful to humane and generous feeling, besides making her dramatically more effec-
tive.

Washington appears in the first and last Scenes,
— thus infolding, as it were, the whole action in
his vast paternal arms; but he is seen for a few
moments only, and at the bottom of the stage,
and is not heard. That the plot failed was re-
motely owing to him; for when, after crossing the
river, as presented in the opening Scene, Arnold
at Peekskill showed him the letter just received
from Beverly Robinson, seemingly on private

business, and asking an interview, Washington, with his habitual masterly prudence and benignant watchfulness, forbade the interview, and this prohibition it was that obliged the more circuitous and more dangerous procedure.

The drama was finished some years since. One Scene, the second of the first Act, was written long ago, and was printed in 1840. The author deems the present a favorable time for the publication of a work which embodies the first American treason, now that our national life has been, and continues to be assailed by the most gigantic and the most wicked treason known to history.

Newport, R. I., December, 1863.

ARNOLD AND ANDRÉ.

———◆———

ACT I.

SCENE I.

The landing at Verplanck's Point on the Hudson River, September 18th, 1780.

Enter, on one side, FLEMING, lame, and VANBERG; on the other, Sergeant BRIGGS, who has lost an arm; with him two farmers.

FLEMING.

Well met, Sergeant Briggs. We are here on the same errand, eh?

BRIGGS.

Aye, cripples that we are. Hard, is it not, to be lazy lookers-on? I'll brook it no longer, now that my stump is healed. There's no snuff like burnt gunpowder: it puts two lives into the brain of a man.

2

FARMER.

And takes one from his arms.

BRIGGS.

Aye, neighbor, that was rare luck, when you see how close the head is to the shoulders. I've my best arm left, and for that one the Commander-in-Chief must find something to do.

FLEMING.

It's certain, then, that he crosses the ferry this afternoon?

BRIGGS.

Certain as the tide. My neighbor here was over at Stony Point two hours ago. The Chief is on his way to Hartford, to confer with the French Commander, Count Rochambeau, lately arrived at Newport. General Arnold has just come down the river to meet him, and will bring him over in a barge.

FLEMING.

Ha! then I shall have another look at General Arnold. There's a general for you, if ever there was one. Could you have seen him at

Behmus's Heights! Like the wind, he was every-where at once, and wherever he came, he blew into us his own heat. That was a time when we drove the Hessians from their encampment. The General and I fell together in the very mouth of the sally-port, wounded in the same leg. I say nothing against General Washington, God bless him; but this I do say, that if Arnold was Commander-in-Chief there would be hotter work and more battles.

BRIGGS.

Stick to your colors, Fleming: that 's right; I like that. But the fewer battles we fight, my friend, the better. In a war like this, to know when *not* to fight is the best generalship. Our retreats have gained us more than our victories. That I learned in the Jersey campaigns. To re-treat is sometimes better even than to beat: it spares ourselves and wears the enemy.

VANBERG.

I perceive, sir, that you are an apt scholar in the school of Washington.

BRIGGS.

And pray, sir, in what school did you learn
the art of war?

VANBERG.

I am myself no soldier, but I had a son killed
at Saratoga, and have another in garrison at
West Point.

BRIGGS.

Your pardon, sir. (*Touching his hat.*) The
father of such sons has a right to his opinions.

VANBERG.

No offence; but our side never was in worse
plight than now. We have been routed in the
South, whence Sir Henry Clinton has just come
back with victorious troops to reënforce New
York. The second French armament, that was
to have been out ere this, is blockaded in Brest.
The first is shut up in Newport. Washington
is too weak to attack New York; 't is as much
as he can do to hold his own on the river. If
we lose West Point, we make our last retreat.

BRIGGS.

Our last retreat will be made by the last man left of us into a bloody grave. But that will never be. We 'll fight them back to the Alleghany Mountains, and hold them there at bay till our sons are big enough to fight in front of us. Oh that I had a hundred arms, instead of but one!

Enter an old man with his grandson, fourteen years of age, and two or three other citizens.

OLD MAN, *to Briggs.*

Can you tell me, sir, is it true that General Washington comes across the ferry this afternoon?

BRIGGS.

He sent word that he is coming. That 's enough : he 'll come, — unless an earthquake swallow up his horse. Him it will not swallow up; for He who makes earthquakes guards his life as the most precious thing on earth at this hour.

OLD MAN.

You have seen him, sir?

BRIGGS.

A hundred times.

OLD MAN.

Is there that greatness in his look, that I have heard speak of?

BRIGGS.

There is that in his aspect that you feel yourself grow larger as you look at him, as a tree grows by looking at the sun. There is in him such a soul, that men get suddenly strong by his side. Have you come to look on him?

OLD MAN.

Aye, sir, and that this boy may have sight of him. His father, my son, is a dragoon in the camp.

BRIGGS.

Ha! Then you shall have speech of him, too, if you wish it. He knows me, and if he did not, this (*striking the stump of his lost arm*) would be a passport to his eye, and from that to his heart.

FLEMING.

There 's the barge !

[*The approaching barge is visible from the stage.*]

BRIGGS.

Aye, so it is, and full of officers. As yet I cannot make them out. Lafayette, the noble young Frenchman, will be among them.

FLEMING.

There 's General Arnold.

OLD MAN.

That 's Washington in the centre, is it not ?

BBIGGS.

Aye, and beside him, on his left, is Lafayette.

FLEMING.

And Arnold is on his right.

BRIGGS.

There, Washington is speaking to Lafayette. The stout one next to Arnold is General Knox of the artillery, a Boston boy. He was a volunteer at Bunker Hill, and has been in every battle in the Jerseys. General Washington likes to have him near himself.

OLD MAN.

Is General Greene, of Rhode Island, there?

BRIGGS.

No. The Commander-in-Chief, while absent, leaves him in command; and worthiest is he to fill so great a place.

FLEMING.

Sergeant, who are the two behind?

BRIGGS.

Ah! now I know them. The one directly behind Lafayette is young Hamilton, whom Washington loves as a son and trusts as a brother. The other is Lee of Virginia, — Major Lee, called Light-horse Harry. He, too, has a place in the heart of the chief. Of these three, Lee, the oldest, is only twenty-four, Lafayette and Hamilton twenty-three.

OLD MAN.

So young and so ripe!

BRIGGS.

They are about to land. Arnold is helping Washington out of the barge.

[*As Washington steps on the shore, Briggs and all the others lift
their hats, which salutation Washington returns, and then,
accompanied by the officers, passes from the stage at the side,
without coming any nearer to the audience. Briggs and the
others go out on the same side, except the Old Man and his
grandson, who remain.*]

GRANDSON.

See, sir; he is speaking to the gentleman
with one arm. But, grandfather, how sad he
looks.

OLD MAN.

Very sad, — very sad. Take that look into
thy heart, my boy: human eyes will never see
a greater.

GRANDSON.

He is mounting his horse.

OLD MAN.

What a majestic air! My son, when you shall
be as old as I am, this hour will be priceless to
your grandchildren, and men will have a joy in
seeing the man who saw Washington.

GRANDSON.

What a fine horse he rides! There he goes.

OLD MAN, *taking off his hat.*

Thank Heaven, I have seen him. What a
man! What a man! [*Exeunt.*

———◆———

SCENE II.

New York..

Sir HENRY CLINTON, *Colonel* ROBINSON, *an Old British Officer.*

SIR H. CLINTON.

Rebellion's tattered banner droops at last,
Wanting the breath of eager confidence.
Discord, twin-brother to defeat, now lifts
Within the Congress walls her husky voice,
(Fit sound for rebel ears,) and in their camp
Lean want breeds discontent and mutiny:
The while, o'er our embattled squadrons poised,
High-crested victory flaps freshened wings,
Fanning the fires of native valiantness.
Quickly shall peace revisit this vext land,
So long bestrid by war, whose iron heel
With her own life-blood madly stains her sides.

ROBINSON.

Our arms' success upon the southern shore, —
Whose thirsty sands are saturate with streams
From rebel wounds, — and the discomfiture
Of new-born hopes of aid from fickle France,
Brought on by Rodney's timely coming, have
Even to the stoutest hearts struck cold dismay.

OLD OFFICER.

Cast down they may be, but despair 's unknown
To their determined spirits. Washington 's
The same as when in '76 he passed
The Delaware, and, in a darker hour
Than this is, rallied his disheartened troops,
And, by a stroke of generalship as shrewd
As bold, back turned the tide of victory.

ROBINSON.

But years of fruitless warfare, sucking up
The people's blood alike and daily substance,
Weigh on th' exhausted land, like helpless debts
Of foilèd enterprise, that clog the step
Of action.

OLD OFFICER.

Deem ye not the spirit dulled
Which first impelled this people to take arms
And brave our mighty power, nor yet extinct
The hope which has their energies upheld
Against such fearful odds. The blood they 've shed
Is blood of martyrs, — consecrated oil, —
Rich fuel to the flame that 's boldly lit
On Freedom's altar, and whose dear perfume,
Upward ascending, is by heroes snuffed,
Strengthening the soul of patriotic love
With ireful vengeance.

SIR H. CLINTON.

Whence, my veteran Colonel,
Comes it, that you, whose scarred body bears
The outward proofs of inward loyalty,
Will entertain for rebels such regard ?

OLD OFFICER.

Custom of war hath not so steeled my heart,
But that its pulse will beat in admiration
Of noble deeds, even those by foemen done ;
Nor does my sworn allegiance to my king

Ban sympathy for men who war for rights
Inherited from British ancestors.

Sir H. Clinton.

Their yet unconquered souls, and the stern front
They have so long opposed in equal strife
To a war-practised soldiery, attest
Their valor; and for us to stint the meed
Of praise for gallant bearing in the field,
Were self-disparagement, seeing that still
They hold at bay our much out-numbering host.
But for the justice of their cause, — the wrong,
Skilled to bedeck itself in garb of right,
Oft cheats the conscience' lax credulity,
And thus will vice, with virtue's armature
Engirt, fight often unabashed. Unloose
The spurs wherewith desire of change, the pride
Of will, hot blood of restless, uncurbed youth
Wanting a distant parent's discipline,
And bad ambition of aspiring chiefs,
Do prick them on to this unnatural war,
And then how tamed would be their fiery mettle,
Heated alone by patriotic warmth.

OLD OFFICER.

My General, I know this people well;
And all the virtues which Old England claims,
As the foundations of her happiness
And greatness, — such as reverence of law
And custom, justice, female chastity,
And, with them, independence, fortitude,
Courage, and sturdiness of purpose, — are
Transplanted here from their maternal soil,
And flourish undegenerate. From these —
Sources exhaustible but with the life
That feeds them — their severe intents take birth,
And draw the lusty sustenance to mould
The limbs and body of their own fulfilment,
So that performance lag not after purpose.
They are our countrymen: they are, as well
In manly resolution as in blood,
The children of our fathers. Washington
Doth ken no other language than the one
We speak; and never did an English tongue
Give voice unto a larger, wiser mind.
You'll task your judgment vainly to descry,

Through all this desperate conflict, in his plans
A flaw, or fault in execution. He
In spirit is unconquerable, as
In genius perfect. Side by side I fought
With him in that disastrous enterprise
Where rash young Braddock fell; and there I
    marked
The veteran's skill contend for mastery
With youthful courage in his wondrous deeds.
Well might the ruthless Indian warrior pause,
Amid his massacre confounded, and
His baffled rifle's aim, till then unerring,
Turn from "that tall young man," and deem in
    awe
That the Great Spirit hovered over him;
For he, of all our mounted officers,
Alone came out unscathed from that dread car-
    nage,
To guard our shattered army's swift retreat.
For years did his majestic form hold place
Upon my mind, stamped in that perilous hour,
In th' image of a stalwart friend, until

I met him next as a resistless foe.
'T was at the fight near Princeton. In quick
    march,
Victorious o'er his van, onward we pressed,
When, moving with firm pace, led by the chief
Himself, their central force encountered us.
One moment paused th' opposing hosts, and
    then
The rattling volley hid the death it bore;
Another, and the sudden cloud, uprolled,
Revealed, midway between the adverse lines,
His drawn sword gleaming high, the chief, — as
    though
That crash of deadly music and the burst
Of sulphurous vapor had from out the earth
Summoned the god of war. Doubly imperilled
He stood unharmed. Like eagles tempest-borne
Rushed to his side his men; and had our souls
And arms with tenfold strength been braced, we
    yet
Had not withstood that onset. Thus does he
Keep ever with occasion even step, —

Now, mockingly before our angry speed
Retreating, tempting us with battle's promise
Only to toil us with a vain pursuit, —
Now, wheeling rapidly about our flanks,
Startling our ears with sudden peal of war,
And fronting in the thickest of the fight
The common soldier's death, stirring the blood
Of faintest hearts to deeds of bravery
By his great presence, — and his every act,
Of heady onslaught as of backward march,
From thoughtful judgment first inferred.

ROBINSON.

If you
Report him truly, and your lavish words
Be not the wings to float a brain-born vision,
But are true heralds who deliver what
In corporal doings will be stern avouched,
Then was this man born to command; and shall
Ingrate revolt be justified by fate,
And Britain's side bleed with the rending off
Of this vast member; they will find it so,
Who seek to gain a greater liberty

Than profiteth man's passion-mastered state.

Jove's bird as soon shall quail his cloud-wet
      plumage,

Sinking his sinewy wafture to the flight

Of common pinions, — or the silent tide

Break its mysterious law at the wind's bidding,

Remitting for a day its mighty flood

Upon this shore, — as that, one recognized

To have all kingly qualities shall not

Assert his natural supremacy,

And weaker men submit to his full sway.

Power doth grow unto the palm that wields it.

The necks that bend to make ambition's seat

Must still uphold its overtopping weight,

Or, moving, be crushed under it.

OLD OFFICER.

                          And heads

That quit the roof of sheltering peace, and bare
      them

To war's fierce lightning for a principle,

Becrown the limbs of men, each one a rock

Baffling with loftiness ambition's step,

Whose ladder is servility.   Were they
Susceptible of usurpation's sway,
This conflict had not been; and then the world
Had missed a Washington, whose greatness is
Of greatness born.   Him have they raised, be-
　　cause
Of his great worth; and he has headed them,
For that they knew to value him.   Had he
Been less, then. they had passed him by; and had
Their souls lacked nobleness, his towering trunk,
Scanted of genial sap, had failed to reach
Its proper altitude.   No smiling time
Is this for hypocritical ambition
To cheat men's minds with virtue's counterfeit.
What made him Washington, makes him the
　　chief
Of this vast league, — and that's INTEGRITY,
The which his noble qualities enlinks
In one great arch, to bear the sudden weight
Of a new cause, and, strengthening ever, hold
Compact 'gainst time's all-whelming step.

SIR H. CLINTON.

        What now
You speak, you'll be reminded of, belike,
Ere many weeks are passed; and well I know,
Your arm will not be backward, if there's need,
To prove your own words' falsity. Meanwhile,
Hold you in readiness for sudden march.

         [*Exit Old Officer.*

ROBINSON.

A better soldier than a prophet.

SIR H. CLINTON.

          Yet,
Scarce does his liberal extolment stretch
Beyond its object's dues. Were Washington
Not rooted in his compeers' confidence,
And in his generalship unmatched, this league
Had long since crumbled from within, and o'er
Its severed bands our arms had quickly triumphed.
In all, his mighty spirit's ordinant.
The while his warriors, ranged in council round
  him,
Listen to plans of learned generalship,

Within the Congress is his voiceless will
Potential as the whitest senator's.
Ever between their reeling cause and us
Comes his stern brow, to awe fell Ruin's spirit.
'T is a grand game he plays, and, by my soul,
Worthy the game and player is the stake.
A fair broad land it is for a new kingdom:
If he can win it, let him wear it. — Still naught
From Arnold? Washington's keen vigilance
Will yet defeat this plot. Delay is fatal.

ROBINSON.

He 's now near Arnold's post. If he depart,
(As 't is his plan, to hold an interview
With the French leaders at the town of Hart-
    ford,)
We 'll know he harbors no suspicious thought;
And then we cannot fail. His presence there
Is hindrance absolute to any movement,
Whether he do suspect or not.

SIR H. CLINTON.

This Arnold, —
That he did vow in hate is warranty

That what he promised he designed to do.
But what then gave him means and power to
    compass
His wishes' end may, too, have changed their
    bent ;
For opportunity, that oftentimes
Creates desire, doth sometimes blunt its edge.
The high command wherewith he has been
    trusted
May heal the wound 't was sought for to re-
    quite.
His now position is a vantage-ground,
Whence he as easily may wipe away
As venge his past disgrace. Beneath his malice
Still burns th' aspiring soldier's love of fame,
Still beats the husband's and the father's heart.

ROBINSON.

There 's in him no live seed of honesty,
For the pure dews of natural affection
To quicken with their sweetness. And the cord,
Wherewith ambitiously he swung himself
Aloft o'er revolution's dark abyss,

Has rotted in his hand; and now he 'd leap
Th' audacious backward leap of desperation.

SIR H. CLINTON.

You know the passes to the fort.   Can he,
Without suspicion of his purposes,
Expose them to our easy mastering ?

ROBINSON.

That can he, and deliver to our hands
The fortress, ere the garrison have time
To counteract their own astonishment.

SIR H. CLINTON.

This post were worth a dozen victories.

ROBINSON.

It is their common magazine, wherein
Are stored munitions for a year's campaign.
To gain it, were to turn into ourselves
A stream of hoarded sustenance for war,
And by diversion of so full a spring,
Wither in them the sinews of contention.

SIR H. CLINTON.

Weak are they now from our late triumphs,
And repetition of unfruitful blows.

The sudden yawning under them of this
Great treachery will strike their souls with awe,
Appall their boldest, and unheart them quite.
Can a resolve, whose execution shall
Flash such quick desolation, lie so deep
That no pale shadow or vague murmur come
Presaging to the general mind? But here
Is André, and in his countenance a light
The prologue to some joyful news.

Enter ANDRÉ.

What bring you?

ANDRÉ.

Tidings that promise to our scheme a quick
And happy consummation. Hear what I
This moment have received:

[*He takes out a letter, and reads as follows :*]

"Our master goes away on the 17th [yesterday] of
this month. He will be absent five or six days. Let
us avail ourselves of this interval to arrange our business. Come immediately and meet me at the lines,
and we will settle definitely the risks and profits of
the copartnership. All will be ready; but this interview is indispensable, and must precede the sailing of
our ship."

SIR H. CLINTON.

Now hold he true, we fail not. Robinson,
What think you? Should he prove a double
    traitor?

ROBINSON.

He dare not, if he would. If that his limbs
Lay at your feet here prostrate with the load
Of chains, more captive were he not to you
Than now he is behind his trenchèd walls.
Whate'er betide, he can't 'scape infamy;
And from no hand but ours receive its price.
Doubly a traitor, he were doubly lost.
His only safety lies in truth to us.

ANDRÉ.

Are we not safe, too, 'gainst his treachery?
We hazard nothing; for our sorest loss
Is but defeat of hope. And if we win,
Our gain is infinite. Not even aught
Of personal peril's in the plan we spoke of.
Seize we the moment, and a wound we give
Shall cleave in twain rebellion's stubborn heart.

ROBINSON:

This interview must be ; or else, no act.

For, 'till he meet us face to face, as still

And secret as a voiceless dream must lie

Within his breast the thought of what he 'd do.

Unto no other ear dare he reveal

The plot or means for its accomplishment.

We must risk something 'gainst his single daring.

The private business that 't is known I have,

Will be our pretext openly to near

His lines, and safeguard afterwards. A flag

Will cover then our meeting.

SIR H. CLINTON.

And meanwhile,

Troops shall embark, and be in readiness

To move on your return. Now despatch, —

And ere thrice thirty hours are passed, I 'll pluck

From wary Washington's high wing a plume,

That shall so maim its flight that to my reach

'T will flutter helplessly.   [*Exeunt.*

ACT II.

SCENE I.

Arnold's Head-quarters.

ARNOLD, *alone.*

So armed is he with foresight, his broad eye
Unknowing balks the cheating future's practice.
He cautioned me against the flag of truce :
To let it pass might kindle now suspicion.
André himself will come ; and he shall meet me
Within our lines. There is no other way.
He 's young and venturesome ; and then his risk
Is small to mine. And I risk naught: my life.
A soldier's life belongs not to himself:
'T is war's light plaything. Mine I 've often cast
Into the cannon's red-mouthed deafening rage.
And for this unconditioned sacrifice,
For trophies, victories, hardships, losses, wounds,
What have I ? Poverty, neglect, injustice.
Defrauded of my pay ; my claims contemned ;

My rank, my sword-won rank, long scanted me.

My power as foe shall teach this wrangling Congress

My worth as friend. England is still my country.

I 've been a rebel; and I 'll do deep penance

For my disloyalty. — But if they win ——

What sound is that? *Arnold the traitor!* Ha!

The traitor Arnold! Are my ears asleep

And dreaming? There! Who spoke? I 'll
 swear I heard it.

And now my eyes abet my ears. See there, —

A multitude of millions, millions, stretching,

Stretching o'er mountains, prairies, endless, endless!

One angry voice from all, *Arnold the traitor!*

'T is false; you lie, you lie; I am no traitor.

I unmake what I 've made. This cause, this
 country,

'T was my soul warmed, 't was my hand built it,
 mine.

I may uproot what I myself have planted. —

But if I fail —— Now is my name emblazoned

High up on Glory's time-proof column, linked
To Washington's.   Too late, 't is now too late.—
Again that fearful sound !   Silence, or I
Go mad.   Am I a baby ?   There, 't is hushed.
I shame to be so shaken.   Ha ! ha ! ha !
What fools imagination makes of us.
Ha ! ha ! ha !

Enter Mrs. Arnold.

MRS. ARNOLD.

What hast thou ?

ARNOLD.

Didst thou hear naught ?

MRS. ARNOLD.

Hear !   Where ?   What ails thee ?

ARNOLD.

Nothing, nothing, nothing.
I 've had ill news again from Congress ; that 's all.

MRS. ARNOLD.

The thankless men !

ARNOLD.

In Philadelphia, tell me,
What didst thou gather ?

MRS. ARNOLD.

That your enemies
Are strong as aye, and still more bitter.

ARNOLD.

Ha !

MRS. ARNOLD.

Some dare to say you are not worth this post.

ARNOLD.

Ha ! say they so ?—(*Aside.*) I 'll prove them
    prophets yet. —
But of the war what 's thought ?

MRS. ARNOLD.

That it cannot last
Much longer. Some, the bolder, say so freely;
Some whisper it; and some, the timid ones,
Shrug up their shoulders and look blank; but all
Are sick of it, and sigh for speedy peace.
While I was there came news of Gates's rout.
Men were aghast. The hopefullest faces fell.
The streets all hissed with railing : some at Gates,
Others at Washington, the most at Congress.
Three out of four are ready for submission ;

And should there come another big defeat,
The Congress will not hold a week together.
Oh, would that chance, which drops us where it
    lists,
Had planted you upon the other side!

ARNOLD.

You 'd have me quit a losing cause ——

MRS. ARNOLD.

Nay, nay.
The cause is yours, for better or for worse.
You 're married to it. So long ago was done
This work of spiteful chance, the seed hath
    grown
To such a stature, that to wrench it now
Would tear up honor by the bleeding roots,
And cast you level with its prostrate trunk.
Oh, no! My maiden hopes, 't is true, were Eng-
    lish;
And I with André and the rest have laughed,
How many a time, — spoilt nursling that I
    was, —
At Continental raggedness and shifts.

But now I'm Arnold's wife; and from the day
That I consented to be that, the cause,
Whereof he is a trusted chief, is mine.
And, know you, I begin to honor it,
To spy a greatness 'hind its shrunken visage.
In Philadelphia my old friends and I,
We angered one another with warm words
And daily contradiction. Washington,
Your friend, our towering head, the man of men,
Even he escapes not their coarse jests and ran-
    cor.
The more they jibed, the more my thoughts
    hugged thee
And our dear boy; and from their banterings
I fled to waking dreams of his great future, —
How his illustrious name will usher him
To eminence in the hard-won Republic;
How in the street people will smile upon him,
And gray-haired men will boast they knew his
    father.
And now I think of it, 't is two days since
Thou hast asked to see him.

ARNOLD.

Is he well?

MRS. ARNOLD.

A lump
Of rosy health, and hourly more like thee.

[*Arnold bursts into tears.*]

Great Heaven! My husband! What hast thou?
thou 'rt ill.

Never before did I behold thee weep.

ARNOLD.

I 'm ill, — to horse, to horse, — I must i' th' air.

Enter an Attendant.

ATTENDANT.

A letter, sir, this moment brought in haste.

ARNOLD.

Ha! from whom?   [*Exit Attendant.*

[*Arnold tears open the letter, and devours its contents.*]

I must away on th' instant.
[*Rushes out.*

MRS. ARNOLD, *gazing at him astounded, and then wildly.*

Ha! — No. — Oh, agony! it cannot be.   [*Exit.*

4

SCENE II.

Cabin of the British sloop-of-war "Vulture," lying in the Hudson River, a few miles below King's Ferry, towards midnight, September 21st.

Colonel ROBINSON, *Major* ANDRÉ, *and Captain* SUTHERLAND, *commander of the "Vulture."*

ANDRÉ.

You'll pardon me, Captain, for thinking, spite of my quarters and my company, that this sailor's life up a river is as tedious as fishing with an unbated hook. It's neither work nor play.

SUTHERLAND.

I am entirely of your mind, Major. It smacks too much of the land-service for my palate. But have patience. Your friend, General Arnold, will soon relieve you.

ANDRÉ.

The General is as cautious in his diplomacy as he is headlong in the field. If he come not to-night, I shall think he has changed his mind.

ROBINSON.

Whether his mind be changed or not, he cannot now retreat. We have too strong a cord round his neck for that.

[*The watch on deck strikes eight bells.*]

ANDRÉ.

What's that? Not midnight.

SUTHERLAND.

Aye, all of it.

OFFICER OF THE WATCH, *on the deck above.*

Boat ahoy!

ROBINSON.

Hark! There he is.

VOICE, *from the boat.*

A friend.

OFFICER, *on deck.*

Where from, and whither bound?

VOICE.

From King's Ferry to Dobbs's Ferry.

OFFICER, *on deck.*

You lubberly land-shark, how dare you, under cover of the night, get within the buoys of one

of His Majesty's ships? Spring your luff and
come along-side, you son of a sea-cook, or I'll
deaden your headway before you can say your
prayers.

ANDRÉ.

A savory salutation that to a major-general.

SUTHERLAND.

That's old Rowley, the best deck-officer in the
service. — Murphy! (*Enter a boy.*) A man has
just come on deck from a boat. Go up and
bring him to the cabin.

MURPHY.

Ay, ay, sir.   [*Exit.*

ROBINSON.

We are not sure that this is Arnold. It will
be prudent for you, Major André, to withdraw
into your state-room.

ANDRÉ.

You were ever a good mentor, Colonel.   [*Exit.*

Enter SMITH.

ROBINSON.

Mr. Smith, I believe.

SMITH.

Colonel Robinson, I 'm glad to see you again.
I bring you a letter from General Arnold.

[*Gives the letter, which Robinson reads.*]

ROBINSON.

Have you any other papers ?

SMITH.

Two passports.

[*Gives them to Robinson.*]

ROBINSON.

This one (*reading*) authorizes you " to go to
Dobbs's Ferry to carry some letters of a private
nature for a gentleman in New York, and to return immediately." The other is a " permission
to Joshua Smith, Mr. John Anderson, and two
servants, to pass and repass the guards near
King's Ferry, at all times." Where is General
Arnold ?

SMITH.

He waits at the landing, where I left him half
an hour since.

ROBINSON.

Mr. Smith, I 'll leave you for a few moments with Captain Sutherland. [*Exit.*

SUTHERLAND.

Take a seat, sir. (*Both sit.*) When do you think, Mr. Smith, this war will end.

SMITH.

When there shall be neither a British soldier on our soil, nor a British gun in our waters.

SUTHERLAND.

Oh! then you prize the war so much, you mean to leave it as an heirloom to your grandchildren?

SMITH.

I give you our final terms, come what may.

SUTHERLAND.

But, seriously, your side looks very black just now.

SMITH.

It has looked black from the first, and looks now blacker than ever; but it is the blackness of the thunder-cloud, — the blacker it is, the more lightning there is in it.

SUTHERLAND.

Well said, by Jove. It can't be denied, there 's good stuff in your fellows. And for my part, Mr. Smith, I tell you frankly, I hate this war, and heartily wish it over, — aye, and I 'll say more, — I wish it over without loss of honor to either side.

SMITH.

I wish, then, from my heart, Captain Sutherland, that you were Prime-Minister of England. Permit me, though, to say, that we might without loss of honor lose our cause; and that would not suit our temper. Honor is a good thing, useful at times, as well as ornamental; but it follows in the wake of our cause, and if we lose that, we shall not take the trouble to pick honor up.

SUTHERLAND.

You count largely on your French allies.

SMITH.

More on their hatred of you than on their love for us.

SUTHERLAND.

They say that General Washington is gone to Hartford to meet the French commanders.

SMITH.

Captain, how many spies do you keep in your service ?

SUTHERLAND.

Always, Mr. Smith, one less than you keep in yours.

Reënter Colonel ROBINSON, *accompanied by Major* ANDRÉ, *in a blue overcoat with cape close buttoned.*

ROBINSON.

Mr. Smith, I am not well enough to go out in an open boat in the night. My friend here, Mr. Anderson, understands the business about which the General and I were to confer, and is ready to accompany you.

SMITH.

The business is yours, Colonel, and not mine. I am but a go-between 'twixt you and the General, happy to serve both of you in any honorable way. It is already so late, I advise that we start at once.

ANDRÉ.

The sooner the better. Farewell, Colonel; fare-well, Captain.

ROBINSON.

God bless you, my friend. Don't forget your instructions.

ANDRÉ.

No fear of that.

ROBINSON.

Farewell.

SMITH.

Gentlemen, good night.   [*Exeunt Smith and André.*

ROBINSON.

This business disquiets me, Captain. I opposed André's going on shore; but he is eager, and would not be overruled. I have misgivings.

SUTHERLAND.

I see no cause for them.

ROBINSON.

Think what a man we are dealing with. Of André's safety what thought will he take who is capable of such a treason?

SUTHERLAND.

But observe how thoughtful he has been of his own safety; and henceforth that is bound closely up with the safety of André.

ROBINSON.

True, but villains are so apt to be botchers; they leave a flaw somewhere, villany so blinds the judgment. From a bad heart there rises into the brain a sickly breath that dims the mind's vision. We will hope for the best.

[*Exeunt.*

———◆———

SCENE III.

Foot of a mountain called the Long Clove, on the western shore of the river, several miles below Stony Point. One hour and a half after midnight, September 22d.

ARNOLD, *alone.*

I like to be alone, and in the night.
Darkness and my deep purpose are attuned;
For that is dark and natural as night,

Aye, and as wholesome too. Wherefore not
    wholesome ?

Strong men are their own law. 'T is meant
    they should be.

Else, wherefore have they that which builds the
    world ?

Poor weaklings pile about their littleness

A rampart of conventions, which the strong

Storm with their intellectual squadrons deep,

Making the garrison slaves irredeemable.

Let them cry shame and conscience as they will.

Conscience, forsooth ! Where are there two alike ?

Fools set their conscience by their neighbors'
    wants.

My wants — they are a liberal hungry crew —

Make mine. Life is a game, where strong will
    wins,

A war, where stratagem and force are victors.

Never from boyhood have I dreaded aught.

Shall I begin so late, and wince with fear

Before the chief of changelings, vile opinion,

The whitest coward of the coward world ?

Traitor! England calls Washington a traitor.
What if I help to prove him one. I hate him,
With his chill stateliness, his wise reserve,
His stubborn prudence, and his calm directness.
Of all the men I've known, only with him
I am not at my ease. It angers me,
To feel my nature is rebuked by his.
A withering frost I'll be to his young greatness,
Striking with palsy their pale bankrupt cause.
In this coarse world failure is ignominy. —
The night wears fast away. 'T is time he came.
Had I been sure of Smith, myself had gone.
It had been quicker done. But he's so vain.
The best of marplots is glib vanity.
The night is cool. I'll walk awhile.   [*Withdraws.*

Enter SMITH *with* ANDRÉ.

SMITH, *cautiously.*

General! General! I left him hereabout. I'll
seek him. He will not be far.   [*Exit.*

ANDRÉ, *alone.*

Moments there are when thought is so ablaze
With all the fires that have inflamed a life,

That memory is one great grasping light,
Flashed on the present from the total past.
I seem not to have lived till now, so burning
Is my new consciousness. 'T is said that men,
In the last agony of drowning, are
Thus flooded with their faded motley years
In one fresh rounded instantaneous picture, —
Life gathering to a point its scattered beams,
To shine its earthly last with warmest flush,
And, robed in full collected brightness, usher
The rising soul to a diviner home.
My mind 's aglow with happiest light, possessed
As by illuminated memories.
There, they are fading, fading fast, like to th' ebb
From blissful clouds of golden beams at evening.
What a vast waking dream! so strangely true, —
A sudden blossomy limning of my life
By beauty's cleansing brush. 'T is going, — gone.
Come back, come back, and wrap me yet awhile
In ——

   [*His arm is grasped by Arnold, who has just reëntered.*]

General Arnold!

ARNOLD.

Major André !

ANDRÉ.

Are we alone ?

ARNOLD.

We are.   A momentous business is this we have to do.   Are you fully empowered.

ANDRÉ.

Fully.   We stand on neutral ground ?

ARNOLD

Aye ; no fear.

Enter SMITH.

SMITH.

General, you know the boat must be sent up the river before daybreak.

ARNOLD.

For that there's time enough.   The boatmen can sleep an hour on their oars.   Let us (*to André*) withdraw a little from the shore.

[*Arnold and André withdraw.*

SMITH, *alone.*

Humph !   He treats me as though I were one

of his corporals. What can he have to say to a Tory that an honest ear might not listen to? Your great men always have secrets. Mystery is the garment of greatness: it helps to keep it warm. But what is to keep me warm? To play sentinel in this air for an hour would give me a tertian, if I had not one already.

Enter ARNOLD.

ARNOLD.

Smith, we can't finish our business here. Send the boat round to the creek, and follow us up to the house.   [*Exit.*

SMITH.

The General's voice is always set to the military pitch. Orders come as glib from his tongue as foul speech from a sailor. Well, I'm thankful to be let off so easily. Colquhoun! (*Calling.*) Colquhoun! These two boatmen brothers make good the saying, Coarse feeders, sound sleepers. Colquhoun! But there's no use in calling. Fellows that snore like the croak of a pond of bull-frogs praying for rain, will not wake before dawn to anything less than a twenty-four pounder. By fist, not tongue, are they to be roused.

[*Exit on the side opposite to that at which Arnold went out.*

———◆———

SCENE IV.

A room in Smith's house, early morning.

Arnold *and* André, *seated at a table with writing materials.* André *in his uniform coat.*

André, *rising.*

They were the last orders Sir Henry Clinton gave me, positive orders, to take no papers.

Arnold, *remains seated.*

Then Sir Henry Clinton cannot take West Point. Have you, Major, the memory of Mithridates ? Can you, by word of mouth, deliver to Sir Henry a plan of the whole system of defences at West Point: the number and calibre of guns in each fort, redoubt, and battery; the construction, size, and strength of each; the amount and quality of the force within the

works ; and the distribution of the several corps
in case of alarm ?   All these details, full, pre-
cise, without error, Sir Henry must have, before
he, with hope of success, can move against a
position so fortified.   Without this key of knowl-
edge, the post remains locked against him in
spite of us both.   Even with it there would be
in the assault some loss of life.   What matters
it whether you risk yours then or now ? it 's for
the same end.   For a soldier, methinks, you cal-
culate adverse chances too curiously.

ANDRÉ.

My life is my King's ; but my honor is my
own.

ARNOLD.

That thought comes to you some hours too
late.

ANDRÉ, *aside.*

The villain is right.

ARNOLD.

Come, Major, be calm.   Your risk is less than
mine ; and see how cool I am.   After all, the

5

danger is not much; and for clearing what there is, trust to chance, or if you like the word better, to Providence.

ANDRÉ, *aside.*

That I should be closely coupled with such a wretch! Ever since I met him, my blood creeps like that of a coward.

ARNOLD.

Pardon me for reminding you of the greatness of your mission. At this moment you are the most important man in His Majesty's service. On your doing well what you were sent to do, hangs the issue of this war. This one success makes your fortune.

ANDRÉ.

Give me the papers.

ARNOLD, *rising.*

There are six of them, (*gives them,*) each one labelled. Those papers are too cheap at ten thousand pounds.

ANDRÉ.

That is the limit of my power.

ARNOLD.

Were I face to face with Sir Henry, he should double that sum. Say to him that I expect it. Now, the sooner he moves the better, and the day must be at once determined. This is Friday, the 22d. In three days, at farthest, Washington will have returned from Hartford. And he will return by West Point to inspect the works: I know him. To that he will give a day, no more; it needs no more; he is no spendthrift of time. In five days from this the coast will be clear. Let Sir Henry move on Tuesday evening. The instant news of your approach reaches the garrison, I will — in so far as I can without causing suspicion — weaken the main points. Under pretence of encountering you, I will send out corps, so separated that they cannot at once aid one the other. They will be stationed in the gorges westward. Keep your main body closer to the river. This I 've already told you : I repeat it ; it is important.

[*A cannon is heard.*]

ANDRÉ, *alarmed.*

What's that? (*Another shot.*) We are betrayed.

Enter SMITH.

ARNOLD.

Smith, what is that firing?

SMITH.

At the " Vulture," from the shore.

ANDRÉ.

But can they reach her? (*Going to the window; cannon-shots continue.*) Ha! that they can. She looks as though she were on fire. There, she is moving.

SMITH, *aside to Arnold, seeing André's uniform.*

What! is he a British officer?

ARNOLD.

Oh, no! A fop of a fellow, a New York cockney, who borrowed a uniform to look big in.

SMITH.

He 'll feel small enough if he is caught in it.

ANDRÉ.

Why, the " Vulture" is dropping down the river! I shall not be able to get back to her.

ARNOLD.

She 'll not have to go far to get out of
reach of those guns. It 's only Colonel Living-
ston keeping his hand in.

SMITH.

And even if the sloop had not budged, the
boatmen will not row out to her again.

ANDRÉ.

But I must be put on board. I demand that.
General Arnold, I have a right to demand so
much.

SMITH.

Young gentleman, if you are a good swimmer,
and a good diver to boot, to dodge the bullets
that might happen to be sent after you, you
may board the sloop.

[*Arnold takes Smith on one side.*]

ANDRÉ.

To be at the mercy of these two! This is no
business for a gentleman. I 've been over-zealous.
So much for playing spy. Spy! Does a spy wear
this coat? No, no! it 's not so bad as that.

[*Arnold and Smith return.*]

ARNOLD.

Mr. Anderson, my friend Smith promises to get you on board, if he can. If not, he will escort you safely beyond our outposts. I'll give you a passport that will be full protection.

ANDRÉ.

I must be content.

ARNOLD, *to André.*

He's bound to me. He'll do the best he can. The hazard's small. The passport will carry you through to your own lines. People are passing to and fro every day. Those papers, — in case of accident, destroy them; then we are both safe. They are the only evidence against us. Not to a soul on our side is the object of this meeting known. For greater secrecy, hide them in your boots. — Mr. Smith, I must return up the river. In your charge I leave Mr. Anderson. — Give my best regards to Colonel Robinson, Mr. Anderson. Tell him the affair shall be settled to suit him. Farewell. (*Coming back.*) Mr. An-

derson, you had better change that borrowed red
coat for a plain one.

[Exeunt, first Arnold on one side, then Smith on the other.

andré, *alone, looking first after Arnold, then after Smith.*
Now that they 're gone, I draw a better breath.
Their presence stifled me. I know not why,
But while they were beside me, it did seem
As they were plotters 'gainst my life. Since
    Arnold
Grasped in the dark upon the shore my arm,
I have not been myself. That touch was ven-
    omed :
It shrivelled up my nerves. I am unmanned ;
I have the conscience of a quaking culprit ;
My fancies are as pale as a sick mother's.
Poh! Poh! A soldier must not let imagination
Unheart him. I have work to do, great work.
He 's right : it can't be done without these war-
    rants.

[He takes out the papers, and seats himself at the table.]

[The curtain drops.]

ACT III.

SCENE I.

Half a mile above Tarrytown, by the road-side among trees, about ten o'clock in the morning of September 23d.

PAULDING, WILLIAMS, *and* VAN WART, *lying on the ground.*

PAULDING.

Did you say, Isaac, that the cow-boys have been seen this week above Pine Bridge ?

VAN WART.

Aye, and felt too ; for they carried off a cow from a Dutch woman three miles beyond the bridge.

WILLIAMS.

The saucy varlets. Why, that 's four or five miles higher up than North Castle, Colonel Jamieson's station. Where was he with his dragoons ?

PAULDING.

Fast asleep. The Colonel is too slow for the

work that's wanted in these parts. I warrant
you, if the marauding rascals come so near to
Captain Boyd, they'll catch a Tartar instead of
a cow.

WILLIAMS.

The skinners, too, have been busy above
White Plains.

PAULDING.

The pirates! They are worse than the cow-
boys. They belong to neither side, and pillage
both. David, what's o'clock, think you? past
nine?

WILLIAMS.

Nearer to ten than nine, I should say, by the
sun.

PAULDING.

This lying down in the daytime is hard both
for bones and brains.

WILLIAMS.

It's the worst work I ever tried; but should
a brace of cattle come along with their noses to
the south, it will pay.

PAULDING.

That's a wise law, that gives cattle for the enemy to the captors. But this waiting on chance is sorry work after all for two-fisted men.

VAN WART.

There comes somebody on horseback, that looks like a gentleman. He has boots on. If you don't know him, Mr. Paulding, you had better make him stop.

Enter Major ANDRÉ *on horseback.*

PAULDING, *who has risen, presents his firelock.*

Stand. Where are you going?

ANDRÉ.

I hope, my friends, you are of our party.

PAULDING.

Which party?

ANDRÉ.

The lower party.

PAULDING.

That's ours.

ANDRÉ.

Then we *are* friends. I am a British officer out on particular business. Let me pass, and take this. (*Offering his watch.*)

PAULDING.

Keep your watch, sir; you must dismount.

ANDRÉ.

Why, what good will it do you to stop me. It may do you harm; for, see here, I have a pass from General Arnold. (*Gives the passport to Paulding, and then dismounts.*) If you detain me, you may get yourselves into trouble. I 'm on my way to Dobbs's Ferry, on the General's business.

PAULDING.

You seem to be a gentleman, sir; and we mean you no harm. But there are bad people about, and in these times it 's hard to tell friend from foe. You must submit to be searched.

WILLIAMS.

Step this way, sir, and take off your clothes.

If you are on an honest errand, no harm will
come to you.

> [*Williams and Van Wart withdraw with André just outside the
> stage.*]

PAULDING.

A British officer, in disguise, with a passport
from General Arnold. That's odd. And how
anxious he seems. When I told him to dismount,
he turned pale. There's something crooked,
which we may be the means of straightening.
(*Reënter Van Wart.*) Do you find any papers?

VAN WART

Nothing; and we've searched him thoroughly.

PAULDING, *going to the side.*

Williams, look into his boots.

WILLIAMS.

There's nothing in this one. (*Showing it, and
turning it upside down.*) — What's that in your
stocking?   Off with it. — Here are papers.
Paulding, you can read.

> [*Gives Paulding the papers.*]

PAULDING.

What 's this ?   Artillery orders at West Point.
And here 's one marked, " Estimate of the
force at West Point and its dependencies."
Williams, search the other foot.   If he is not a
spy, I don't know how to read.

WILLIAMS.

Here are three more.

[*Gives them to Paulding.*]

PAULDING, *reading.*

" Report of a Council of War on the Cam-
paign."   " Description of the works at West
Point."   There 's treason, somewhere, — nothing
less.   Some black plot.   What a providence that
we were at this very spot at this very hour!
Keep your eye on him, Isaac.   He 's a prize.
We must take him right off to North Castle.
That 's the nearest station.

[*André, who has re-dressed, advances.   Paulding and the other
two talk low apart.*]

ANDRÉ, *aside.*

Sooner or later a curse doth ever follow false-

hood. How quick it falls on me. Till now my
life was true. This is my first lie, and I am
caught in it, — caught acting a monstrous falsehood. Oh, what a fool I 've been! They
should have chosen some sharper, harder instru-
ment for such a work. — I blame no one but
myself. — What will be my fate? — I dare not
think of it.

[*Rests his head against a tree.*]

PAULDING.

I tell you, this is a great day's work. Few of
the generals have done a better.

WILLIAMS.

Think you so?

PAULDING.

Aye. Had that man got to New York with
those papers, in a week the English would have
had West Point. And then, good bye to our
cause.

VAN WART.

Indeed!

PAULDING.

Mark me : when this republic shall have grown great, — which it will do faster than ever yet a nation on the earth, — and shall be as strong as old England herself ——

WILLIAMS.

As strong as England !

PAULDING.

Aye, it will take but two or three generations for that ; — for this day's doings, tens of millions will know the names of us three, and speak them with thanks, and will hand them down to be blessed by their children's children, to the twentieth generation ; and on this very spot where we stand will gather a great crowd, — which our children may live to see, — and raise a monument to our memory.

VAN WART.

What ! a monument !

PAULDING.

Aye. And thereon, in large, deep letters, your name, Isaac, will be cut. Now to our prisoner.

See how he 's troubled. I should n't wonder if
he turns out to be a British general.

WILLIAMS, *to André.*

Now, what will you give us to let you go?

ANDRÉ.

Anything you name.

WILLIAMS.

Will you give your horse, saddle, bridle, watch,
and one hundred guineas?

ANDRÉ.

And a hundred apiece to each of you besides,
and as much more in dry goods, and have them
delivered at this very spot, or anywhere that you
shall name.

PAULDING.

Not for ten thousand guineas would we let you
go. Here is some dark plot against the American
cause, and you, Mr. Anderson, as your passport
calls you, are an agent in it. Had you this passport directly from General Arnold's hand?

ANDRÉ.

Ask me no questions.

PAULDING.

When did you see General Arnold?

ANDRÉ.

Bring me to one of your commanders. To
him I will reveal all.

PAULDING.

Forward, then, to North Castle.   [*Exeunt.*

———◆———

SCENE II.

*Arnold's Head-quarters, opposite West Point, September
25th.   Breakfast-table set for ten or eleven persons.*

ARNOLD, *Mrs.* ARNOLD, *Major* VARICK, *Arnold's aide-de-camp.*

MRS. ARNOLD.

Husband, he sent direct word that with his
suite he would be here to breakfast?

ARNOLD.

Yes; and the Commander-in-Chief is an early
riser. You'll hear their tramp presently. Had
he named the hour, we should be sure of him:
he is the most punctual man in his camp. Ah!

6

here he is. (*Enter Colonel Hamilton and Major McHenry.*) Welcome, gentlemen. Where 's the General ?

HAMILTON.

He turned off towards the river, to inspect the works before dismounting. He sends us to request that you will not wait breakfast for him.

ARNOLD.

Mrs. Arnold, this is Colonel Alexander Hamilton, aide-de-camp to General Washington ; Major McHenry, aide-de-camp to the Marquis Lafayette. The orders of the Commander-in-Chief, whatever they may be, must be obeyed; so, we will go to breakfast. Come, gentlemen. (*All sit at the table.*) This ride to Hartford has been a pleasant holiday to you. How did you like our French allies ?

HAMILTON.

We liked them much. But what we like even better than them is the effect the interview with Count Rochambeau has had on General Washington. We all observe that he is less silent and more cheerful since we left Hartford than on the journey thither.

ARNOLD.

What is the amount of the land-force the Count has brought over?

McHENRY.

Between six and seven thousand choice troops.

ARNOLD.

Any artillery?

McHENRY.

A larger train than belongs to such a force; both heavy and light guns.

[*Enter an Attendant, who gives Arnold a letter, and retires.*]

ARNOLD, *who with difficulty conceals his emotion while reading the letter.*

I am called, gentlemen, across the river to West Point. Say to General Washington that I have been suddenly summoned on business. [*Exit.*

HAMILTON.

The General, I fear, has had bad news. That letter seemed to disturb him. ·

MRS. ARNOLD.

I thought so too.

[*Enter an Attendant and whispers to Mrs. Arnold, who hastily
quits the room, followed by the Attendant.*]

HAMILTON.

Our host and hostess being both called away,
let us, gentlemen, seek the party on horseback.

VARICK.

With all my heart. It is some time since I
saw the Commander-in-Chief. [*Exeunt.*

————◆————

SCENE III.

Mrs. Arnold's chamber; a cradle near the bed.

ARNOLD, *then Mrs.* ARNOLD.

MRS. ARNOLD.

What is it? Thou 'rt pale!

ARNOLD.

We must part on the instant, — perhaps for-
ever.

MRS. ARNOLD.

Part! Oh, Heaven! what mean'st thou?

ARNOLD.

I 've played a bold game and lost. My life is
forfeit.

MRS. ARNOLD.

Thy life!

ARNOLD.

Unless I reach the enemy's lines, I 'm lost.

MRS. ARNOLD.

The enemy! Oh, my fears! Thou art lost
indeed. Why didst thou not confide in me,
thy wife? Thou didst repulse me. I never
had betrayed thee, — I might have saved thee.
And my boy! (*Throws herself on her knees before the cradle.*) Oh, my poor child!

ARNOLD.

I must be gone.

MRS. ARNOLD.

Tell me all. I yet may save thee.

ARNOLD.

Too late, too late. André's taken.

MRS. ARNOLD.

André!

ARNOLD.

Farewell! Farewell! My very life-blood ebbs with every minute lost.

MRS. ARNOLD.

I 'll go with thee. And our boy. Wilt thou desert us?

ARNOLD.

Wilt thou see me die?

MRS. ARNOLD.

Fly! fly! Away! away!

[*Arnold kisses the child and then embraces her. She swoons in his arms.*]

ARNOLD.

Great Heaven! she faints. And I must leave her thus! (*Lays her on the bed.*) Wife! Wife! Oh, wretch that I am!   [*Rushes out.*

SCENE IV.

Head-quarters of General Washington, at Tappan, September 30th. Street in the village.

Enter Colonel Hamilton, *aide-de-camp to Washington, and Major* Varick, *aid to Arnold.*

HAMILTON.

He dies to-morrow.

VARICK.

Has the Commander-in-Chief signed the sentence?

HAMILTON.

Not yet. He will sign it to-day. 'T is the hardest duty he ever had to do.

VARICK.

What a fate for a young, generous gentleman!

HAMILTON.

As bitter to him, poor fellow, as his capture was to us providentially merciful. A full, fair trial he has had by a jury, than which one more enlightened and honorable never gave a verdict. Six Major-Generals, — Greene, President, and with him, Stirling, St. Clair, Lafayette, Howe, Steuben ; and eight Brigadiers, — Parsons, Clinton, Knox, Glover, Patterson, Hand, Huntington, Stark. To justice never was given by a tribunal a stronger bond than that sealed by the character of these fourteen officers.

VARICK.

Was there no dissentient voice ?

HAMILTON.

Finally, none. Two or three members of the board, prompted by humanity, started some technical objections, but could not sustain them. André bears his doom like a soldier, and, by his gentleness and dignity, wins all who approach him.

VARICK.

In battle how light a thing it is to give or take death. But in calm blood, by deliberate judgment to cut off the life of a fellow-being, — the brain trembles over its work. The thought of André must light a hell in Arnold's breast.

HAMILTON.

In his breast there is not glow enough to
kindle the fires of conscience. His nature is
ruthless and shameless. Think of his writing a
defiant, threatening letter to the Commander-in-
Chief.

Enter Sergeant BRIGGS, *accompanied by another sergeant.*

BRIGGS.

Can you tell me, Colonel Hamilton, has General Washington signed the sentence?

HAMILTON

Not yet.

BRIGGS.

But he will sign it?

HAMILTON.

'T is said he will.

BRIGGS.

I knew he would.

HAMILTON.

How did you know it?

BRIGGS.

Because he ought to sign it; and *he* never yet

failed, and never will fail, to do what he ought
to do.

HAMILTON.

Some think he ought not to sign it.

BRIGGS.

Tories and traitors and love-sick girls.

HAMILTON.

Sergeant, you seem much moved.

BRIGGS.

Moved! I have n't slept for a week for dreaming. The instant I close my eyes, I see the
cursed red-coats pouring up the heights, — our
men scattered and flying, shot down like rab-
bits, — officers bewildered, — all dismayed, all betrayed. They 've scaled Fort Putnam! There!
the royal ensign waves above it! And that
wakes me; and I cry for joy to find I 've
been dreaming. I shall do nothing but dream
o' nights while André lives. But there 's one
condition on which I 'd spare his life.

HAMILTON.

What 's that?

BRIGGS.

Their giving us Arnold in his place. Oh, for
that, I 'd hug André with my one arm. I have
but the one ; but look you, Colonel, I 'll lay it on
a block, and you may hew it off inch by inch to
the shoulder, if thereby we can clutch that —
what shall I say — traitor! There have been
traitors before ; but Arnold is something diaboli-
cally new.

VARICK.

Now that his villany is baffled, what have we
to gain by taking the life of poor André ?

BRIGGS.

Poor André, — what to gain ? I knew a man,
a brave one. I saw him fight at Princeton, — a
young, strong man and true. He left a wife and
babe at home in Monmouth. The day before
yesterday came a letter telling him his wife was
ill unto death. No mother, no sister, no brother,
near her. The poor man was beside himself with
grief. In that state he deserted. He was taken ;
and yesterday, within twelve hours of his capture,

he was shot; and it was right that he was,—it
was right. And a British officer, by the British
Commander-in-Chief sent with most malignant
purpose, comes within our lines under a false
name, under a false character, in disguise, at
midnight, to plot with the worst enemy our cause
could have,—to plot the ruin of that cause by
one great perfidious blow,—goes away in the
dark, hiding in his boots the plans and papers to
make that blow unfailing; this man, who came
upon us stealthily, like a thief in the night, and
went out like a thief in the night, carrying with
him a key to our very citadel of safety,—a man,
who, by means gotten through his own double,
treble falsehood and the deep treason of his black
accomplice, would, within a week, have compassed
the stronghold of our territory, shattered our army,
struck despair to the whole country's heart, perhaps, aye, quite possibly, made captive Washington himself,—this man,—this man is poor André!
Hanging 's too good for him.

> [*Exit, followed by his companion, who makes an energetic ges-
> ture of sympathy and approval.*

VARICK.

Colonel, there's marrow in that man's bones.

HAMILTON.

Aye, Major; that's the stuff that carried us into this war, and will carry us through it.

[*Exeunt.*

———◆———

SCENE V.

A Hall.

At the farther end General WASHINGTON, *seated at a table, with his face to the audience, takes a pen. The fourteen Generals who formed the Board of Inquiry that sat on André are standing about the table on his right and left, looking at him sign the sentence, which he does. He then rises, gives the paper to General* GREENE, *President of the Board, bows to the Generals and retires, they all bowing deferentially.*

GREENE.

His heaving breast made the weak pen to tremble,
Until he ruled it with his mighty will.

LAFAYETTE.

Tears are rare visitors to those calm eyes;

And when they come, they bring a solemn mes-
    sage
From the great heart that could no longer quench
    them.

KNOX.

But once before have I beheld him thus.

STEUBEN.

And yet, at last, in what a clear firm hand
He wrote the one irrevocable word,
His loved and dreaded name.

GREENE.

               The steady hand
Belongs to war, to peace the moistened eye.
War dislocates the man, his sterner half
Ruling the gentler with the soldier's law,
Which is sharp as his sword, quick as his flint.

KNOX.

The law of war is now our law of life.
Its rough necessities so sway the hour
That in a case like this mercy were suicide.

LAFAYETTE.

As if by miracle we have escaped

The ruin of the noblest, grandest cause
That e'er by power of truth and manliness
Was launched upon the storms of rageful war.

GREENE.

By providential blessing we 've escaped ;
But while from danger's loosened grip our hearts
Still shudder, round beneath us baffled Death
From rock to rock, in sight, springs black and
    bellowing,
Where the loud foam of open enmity
Curls o'er the silent reefs of treason deep;
So that, to ward the costliest wreck e'er strewn
Upon the shores of time, we still must bind
In one great cable all our life's best threads,
And on our haughty foe hurl death for death.

THE END.